GOD CARES WHEN I'M FEELING MEAN

BY ELSPETH CAMPBELL MURPHY
ILLUSTRATED BY JANE E. NELSON

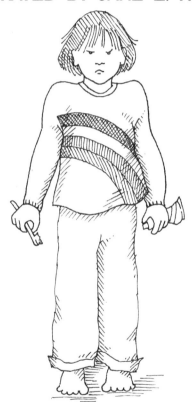

Chariot Books

from David C. Cook Publishing Co.

GOD CARES WHEN I'M FEELING MEAN

BY ELSPETH CAMPBELL MURPHY
ILLUSTRATED BY JANE E. NELSON

Chariot Books is an imprint of the David C. Cook Publishing Co.
David C. Cook Publishing Co., Elgin, Illinois 60120
David C. Cook Publishing Co., Weston, Ontario

GOD CARES WHEN I'M FEELING MEAN
First Printing, 1984
Printed in the United States of America
89 88 87 86   5 4 3 2

Library of Congress Cataloging in Publication Data
Murphy, Elspeth Campbell.
   God cares when I'm feeling mean.

   Summary: A child asks God's help to come to terms with
the times that she feels and acts mean.

   1. Children's stories, American. [1. Conduct of life—
Fiction. 2. Christian life—Fiction] I. Nelson, Jane E., ill. II.
Title.
PZ7.M95316Gnc 1984   [E]   83-72501
ISBN 0-89191-789-6

I woke up mean this morning, God.
I saw myself in the mirror,
and even my hair looked crabby.
"Grrrarhrr!" I said.
I squeezed the toothpaste tube so hard
that toothpaste squirted all over everything.
That just made me madder.

When my mother called me for breakfast,
I stomped downstairs as hard as I could.
"I don't believe it!"
I yelled as soon as I got to the table.
"You got the wrong cereal!
I told you I needed Oatsey Crunchies,
but you got Crunchy Corn Curls.
Yuck! Gag!"
"That's no way to talk," said my father sternly.
I knew it wasn't, God, but I was feeling mean.

4

5

That's why I stole the bananas
off my baby brother's cereal
when no one was looking.
He's stuck in that stupid high chair,
so I knew he couldn't get back at me.
But—wouldn't you know it—he started to scream.
"What did you do?" my mother asked me.
"Why do you always blame *me*?" I said.

This was not turning out to be a good day, God. But that's how it happens when you wake up mean and act mean.

Things just get worse and worse.

Things sure didn't get any better
when my friend picked me up for choir practice.
She was happy,
because she had a beautiful, new red jacket.
But I was feeling mean,
so I said that her jacket looked like a boy's jacket.

She didn't even want to wear it after that.
I knew how she felt,
because I would have felt awful
if she'd said that to me.
"I'm sorry," I said quietly.
"Your jacket looks pretty—
it doesn't look like boys' clothes.
I just said that to be mean."

But you know what, God?
As soon as I said something nice,
I didn't feel quite so mean anymore.

When I got home later,
my brother was in his playpen,
because my parents were working.

18

David the shepherd boy

WHERE ARE YOU, G
PSALM 139 FOR CHILDREN
BY ELSPETH CAMPBELL
ILLUSTRI. BY JANE E. KUM

I asked my mother if I could take him out, and she said yes—if I promised to watch him and play nice.
You know what, God?
When I was taking care of my brother, I didn't feel like being mean to him anymore.

And then I helped my father with lunch
without even being asked.
I told him when I grow up
I would rather have a nice kid
than a mean one.
And he laughed and said, "That's for sure!"

20

I don't know why I wake up feeling mean some days, God.
But I know how you want me to *act*, no matter how I *feel*.
Because it's the same for the great days
and the so-so days—
and even the rotten days.

You tell me in your Word:

"Do to others
as you would have them
do to you."

LUKE 6:31*

This verse is found on page ____ in my Bible.

*This text is taken from the New International Version, but
you may use the version of your choice.

Dear Parents and Teachers,

When was the last time your child hummed the song from a McDonald's, Kentucky Fried Chicken, or Coca-Cola commercial? Children pick up jingles so quickly that soon they can sing the entire advertisement perfectly—complete with motions and intonation. The fact that the words stick in their minds—and pop out of their mouths at the most unexpected moments—shows how easily children memorize.

Your children can memorize Scripture with the same ease, if you read Bible passages with them and help them understand the message. As you read this book together, children will capture truths and promises that will stay with them throughout their lives. God will bring these good words to their minds over and over again—right when they need to hear them! This is one way God lets his children know he's always with them.

The following steps will help you teach your child to memorize. Instead of trying to do all seven at one sitting, we suggest you spread them out over several days or weeks. We want children to associate the Bible with relaxed and happy times, so avoid pressure and tension.

1. Memorize the passage yourself. Read it in several translations and meditate on its meaning for you and for your children.

2. Read this book with your children several times. You'll be surprised how quickly they memorize without even trying. If you are using a version other than the New International Version, substitute it each time you read the book.

3. Help your children locate the passage in their own Bibles. Have them underline the verses with a colored pencil and mark the spot with a bookmark. Your children can write the Bible page number in the line on page 23.

4. Read the passage with your children and have them repeat each line after you.

5. Read the passage line by line again. This time, define unfamiliar words and phrases. Ask your children to explain the passage in their own words, and help them to think of times when knowing this passage by heart would encourage them.

6. Read the passage through several more times, each time having the children repeat more lines after you until they can say the whole passage themselves.

7. Review the passage with your children once a day for a while, then once a week, then once a month. Say the passage with your children whenever an appropriate occasion arises.